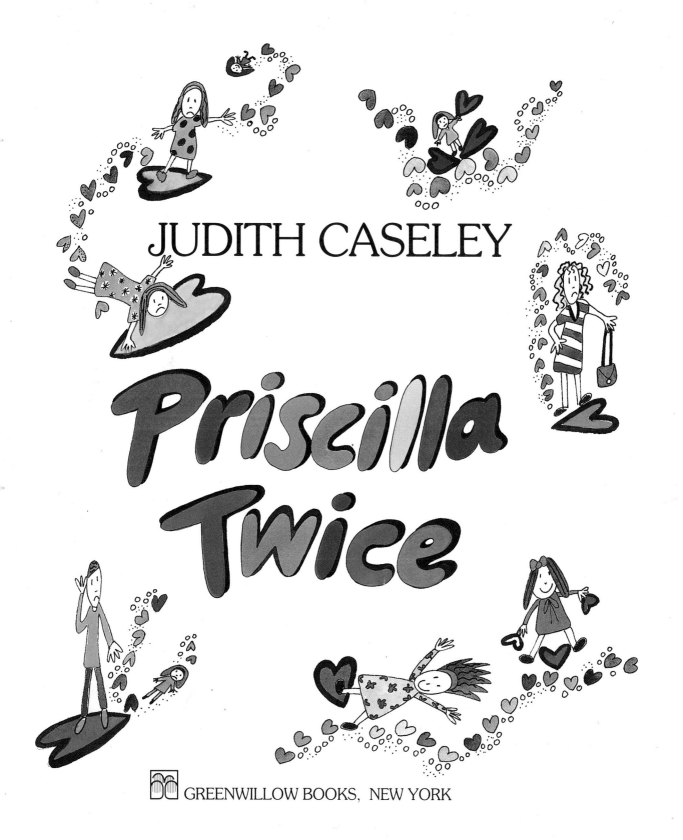

JUDITH CASELEY

Priscilla Twice

GREENWILLOW BOOKS, NEW YORK

Watercolor paints and colored pencils were used for the full-color artwork.
The text type is Souvenir.

Printed in Singapore by KHL Printing Co. Pte. Ltd.
First Edition   10 9 8 7 6 5 4 3 2 1

LIBRARY OF CONGRESS CATALOGING-IN-PUBLICATION DATA
Caseley, Judith.
Priscilla twice / by Judith Caseley.
p.   cm.
Summary: When Priscilla's parents divorce, she learns that there
are different kinds of families.
ISBN 0-688-13305-3 (trade).   ISBN 0-688-13306-1 (lib. bdg.)
[1. Divorce—Fiction.]   I. Title.   PZ7.C2677Pr   1995
[E]—dc20   94-12988   CIP   AC

For Ava,

with love

and thanks

When Priscilla's teacher told the children to draw pictures of their families, Priscilla put her mama on one side of the paper and her papa on the other.

"Where are you, Priscilla?" said the teacher.

"Oh," said Priscilla. "I forgot."

So Priscilla started over and drew herself twice. She made a teensy tiny Priscilla on the side with her mother, and a speck of a Priscilla on the side with her father.

"You're awfully small," said the teacher.

"It doesn't matter," said Priscilla.

"And you've drawn yourself twice," said the teacher.

"They both need me," Priscilla answered.

After school Priscilla's mother invited
Abby over for a play date. They did their
homework together in Priscilla's room
and played with their favorite dolls.

Priscilla's father came home from work.
"Hello, Sweet Pea Priscilla!" he said to his daughter.
It was the name he had given her when
she was a baby.
"Hello, String Bean Papa," said Priscilla. It was the
name she had given him when she'd learned to talk.
"What's your mother's nickname?" said Abby.
"I haven't given her one yet," said Priscilla.

They all had dinner on the yellow kitchen table. Priscilla's mother asked them about school. Priscilla's father asked them about the dinosaurs they were studying. But Priscilla's father didn't talk to Priscilla's mother, and Priscilla's mother didn't talk to Priscilla's father.

Back in her bedroom Priscilla brushed Abby's hair.
"My mother gives my hair one hundred strokes
every night before I go to bed," said Priscilla.
"Your mother is nice," said Abby. "But how
come she doesn't talk to your father?"
"It's quieter that way," said Priscilla.

But after Abby went home that night,
when Priscilla's father tucked her into
bed, she said, "How come you don't
talk to Mama anymore?"
"Ruth!" called Priscilla's father, and her
mother came in, and her father said,
"It's time to tell her."
Priscilla's mother sat down and hugged
her. "Papa and I are going to get a
divorce," she said. "We can't live together
anymore. But both of us will always
love you, and nothing will change that."
"Nothing?" said Priscilla.
"Nothing," said her father and mother.

The next morning Priscilla made
her bed as neatly as possible.
She ate all of her oatmeal without
asking for more brown sugar
and drank every drop of milk.
She cleared her breakfast dishes.
After school she took off her
school clothes and did her
homework without being asked.
She set the table for supper
and brushed her teeth
after dinner.

"Sweet Pea Priscilla," said her father when he
tucked her into bed, "I hear you were
a perfect angel today."
"String Bean Papa," said Priscilla,
"if I keep my
room clean and
behave myself,
maybe you
won't have
to get a
divorce."
"Ruth!"
called
her father,
and her mother
came in and told
Priscilla that getting a
divorce had nothing to do with
cleaning her room or behaving herself.
"It has nothing to do with you," said her mother.
"Nothing?" said Priscilla.
"Nothing," said her mother and father.

Priscilla's father moved out of
the house and down the street.
He took his favorite armchair with
him, his bookcase full of books,
and the yellow kitchen table.

"It's not the same as home," said Priscilla, eating her first peanut butter and jelly sandwich at the yellow kitchen table in her father's new apartment.

"It's the same table," said her father.

"It's not the same family," said Priscilla. "And my sandwich tastes different."

"I'll ask your mother what brand of peanut butter you like," said her father.

"The all-together-family brand," said Priscilla.

Her father tucked her into bed. "You're still my Sweet Pea Priscilla," he said to her. "I love you more than ever."

"You're not my String Bean Papa anymore," said Priscilla. "It's just not the same."

Priscilla spent one week with her father
and the next week with her mother.

She had two sets of toys and books and two sets
of clothes and two toothbrushes and two places
for her friends to play.

On play dates Abby liked the way Priscilla's
father cooked. "He makes creamier macaroni
and cheese than your mother."
"My mother lets me stay up later," said Priscilla.

"Your father bought you lots of new toys,"
said Abby.
"My mother doesn't want to spoil me,"
said Priscilla.

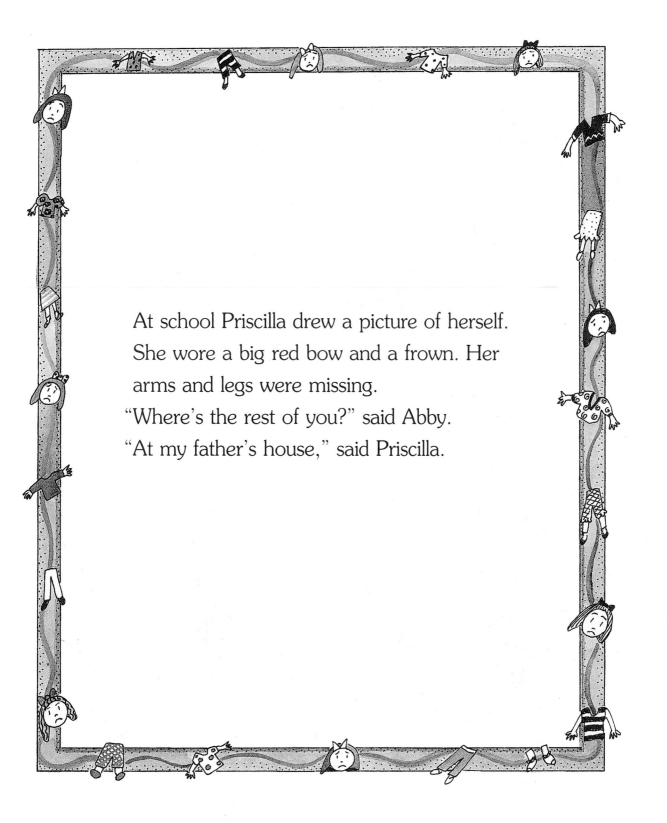

At school Priscilla drew a picture of herself.
She wore a big red bow and a frown. Her
arms and legs were missing.
"Where's the rest of you?" said Abby.
"At my father's house," said Priscilla.

The week she spent at her mother's house, Priscilla left her bed messy and threw her dolls on the floor and asked for ice cream for breakfast and told her mother that she made the worst macaroni and cheese in the world. "Papa makes it a thousand million times better," she said as her mother brushed her hair a hundred times.

"My little angel," said her mother, laughing. "I'll get the recipe from your father."

"I'm not an angel," said Priscilla.

"Isn't it the truth?" said her mother. "I love you when you're messy and horrid and when you hate my macaroni. And you can't make me stop."

The week she spent at her father's house, Priscilla refused to take a bath. She put red nail polish on her dolls, and shaving cream on the Jell-O to make it look pretty.

Her father gave her a hug and said, "You smell like a skunk because you won't take a bath. You ruined my Jell-O, and your dolls have red fingertips. But I love you more than ever."

"Give Mama the recipe for your macaroni and cheese," said Priscilla. "Abby likes yours better."

The days and weeks passed.
At school one morning Priscilla divided her
paper down the middle. On one side she drew
a picture of herself with her father, sitting down
to dinner at the yellow kitchen table. Hearts
were dancing on their heads, because her father
loved her. She called it String Bean Papa and
Sweet Pea Priscilla.

On the other side she drew herself with her mother,
sitting at their new kitchen table eating plates of
macaroni. Hearts were dancing on their heads.
She called it Sweet Pea Priscilla and Macaroni Mama,
because her mother loved her and had gotten the recipe
from her father. Priscilla told her teacher that there were
different kinds of families. Her teacher agreed, and then

Priscilla drew
a few more hearts
on each side
of the picture.